Focus on the Family®

PRESENTS

McGEE™ and me!

Do the Bright Thing

Bill Myers

Based on characters created by Bill Myers and Ken C. Johnson, and the teleplay by Ken C. Johnson.

Tyndale House Publishers, Inc.
Wheaton, Illinois

For Mary Ann Bedard,
David King,
Cindi Remington,
Jenny Williams,
Maria Varni,
Laurie Leinonen,
and Beth Knutson—
Some hardworking past and present McGeeites.

Front cover illustration copyright © 1990 by Morgan Weistling
Interior illustrations by Nathan Greene, copyright © 1990 by
Tyndale House Publishers, Inc.

Library of Congress Catalog Card Number 90-70610
ISBN 0-8423-4112-9
McGee and Me!, McGee, and *McGee and Me!* logo are trademarks
of Living Bibles International
Copyright © 1990 by Living Bibles International

00   99   98   97
 8   7   6   5

Contents

Now teach me good judgment as well as knowledge. For your laws are my guide. (Psalm 119:66, *The Living Bible*)

ONE
Professor Gizmo

I strapped my breathtakingly beautiful body into the Photon Combustion Accelerator and began switching switches, dialing dials, and knobbing knobs. Faster than you could say, "Oh no! What's this incurably cute and contagiously clever cartoon character concocting this time?" the Accelerator crackled to life.

Yes, it is I—Professor Pepto Gizmo—world-famous inventor and frozen yogurt connoisseur.

Now, it's true, my inventions haven't always been the success I'd hoped. Like my remote-controlled, solar-powered umbrella opener. Hey, don't laugh. It was terrific, except for the fact that it only worked when the sun was out. Then there was my fully automatic, jet-powered tooth flosser. Again, a terrific success, except that it occasionally yanked out a tooth. (The public can be so picky sometimes.)

All of that was behind me now (except for the dental bills). Now it was time to test my crowning achievement. The concept was simplistically simple. Every night for years those glitzy and glamorous TV stars had traveled on the air waves all the way

9

across the country to my TV set, just so I could see them in my living room. It didn't seem fair. I mean, if we were such good friends I should have to go to their homes once in a while, too.

Well! My handy-dandy Photon Accelerator would change all of that. I pushed the thrust energizers all the way forward to "Here Goes Nothin'" and grabbed the remote control to my TV. I smiled as I imagined myself landing right in the middle of all my favorite TV stars (who, of course, would be flocking around me to applaud my genius). I pressed the button, and Crackle-Zzzzzzt-Pop! I was transported into Video Land.

I looked around. Hey, wait a minute! Something was wrong! A quick glance at the remote explained it: someone had set the channel selector to the wrong station! I wasn't surrounded by stars. Instead, I was riding the back of some bird who was singing about the letter H and the number 9. The only thing stranger than the song was the bird—he was huge and yellow and couldn't sing on key if his life depended on it!

I leaped from his back and landed on a front porch, just in time for this blue furball to start chasing me all over the place screaming, "Me want cookie. . . . Me want cookie!" Hey, cookies sounded good—and normally I would have stuck around for a bite to eat—but I had this sneaking suspicion that the furball's "bite" was gonna be me.

I ran up the steps, only to be met by this weird guy with a Dracula-type accent. I grabbed his arm and asked, "Where am I? Where am I?" But all he did was count the number of times I asked the question.

"Dat's vun 'Vhere am I'. . . . Dat's two 'Vhere am I's,' ah-ha-ha-ha."

Suddenly I heard an argument behind me. I spun around just in time to see the letters K and O punching it out. I tell you, on a weirdness scale of 1 to 10, this place was definitely an 11. It was too much, even for me. So I grabbed the remote control and pushed another channel.

Zzzzzt-pop-click!

Now where was I? Let's see. . . . There were a couple of Mom-and-Pop types standing around in a kitchen that looked like it was right out of the fifties. Come to think of it, the Mom and Pop kinda looked like they came out of the fifties, too!

Best I could figure, they were either forest rangers or they worked at a zoo, 'cause all they did was talk about this Beaver. Everything was "the Beaver this," "the Beaver that." It's like he was practically part of the family or something. He even had his own room upstairs!

Now don't get me wrong, I'm all for animal rights and everything. But what was gonna happen when ol' Beaver boy decided to start building dams in the bathtub?

Oh, and there was one other problem. As nice as Momsie and Popsie were, there was no getting around one cold, hard fact: these folks were boring. I mean, they made memorizing multiplication tables seem like a trip to Disneyworld.

"Come on folks!" I hollered. "How 'bout a little ac tion, a little drama?"

They smiled at me blankly.

"Don't you guys ever argue? Don't you ever fight?"

"Ah," Mom nodded, seeming to understand. "How about some cookies and a glass of nice warm milk? Wally will be home soon and—"

"No, no, no!" I shouted, feeling myself getting a little hot under the collar. "Action! Drama! DOESN'T ANYTHING EVER HAPPEN AROUND HERE??!!"

It was no use. They just didn't understand. So before they could suggest we sit at the table for a nice, long, boring talk about the problem . . .

Zzzzt-pop-click! I hit the channel selector.

Sizzling smoke rings! I must have landed in the middle of a gigantic fire! Everywhere I looked there was smoke and smog. I mean, either I was in a gigantic fire, or I was in downtown Los Angeles.

But hold it! In front of me were a zillion screaming crazies. Each and every one was jumping up and down. They were shrieking and dancing for all they were worth (which couldn't have been more than 25 cents, judging from the way they looked). Apparently I'd stumbled upon some primitive stone-age tribe carrying out their crazed, sacrificial rituals. I figured I must have made my way into a National Geographic Special. But my fancy figuring proved faulty.

Suddenly there was a tremendous explosion behind me—so loud that it knocked me to my knees. Actually, it wasn't an explosion. It was a roar. A roar that wouldn't stop. A roar that drove the natives even crazier.

I spun around just in time to see four strange and eerie creatures . . . aliens! I mean, these guys looked worse than E.T.!

One of the mutants was behind a control panel that looked a lot like a keyboard. Another one was behind what appeared to be a set of drums. Two others were holding strange-looking weapons disguised as guitars. But they couldn't be guitars. Guitars couldn't possibly make the awful noise these things made! They had to be some sort of living organisms that the aliens were tormenting. You could tell by their ghastly screeches and growls that the poor guitar-shaped creatures were not happy campers.

Thick, gagging smoke . . . crazed natives . . . brain-breaking blasts . . . out-of-control aliens . . . Where was I? Had I stumbled into somebody's nightmare? Had I discovered a TV station from beyond?

I glanced down at the channel zapper. Oh! Silly me! I'd accidentally punched up MTV!

Quicker than you could say, "Got a couple of aspirin?" I hit the road by hitting the last and final channel.

Zzzzzt-pop-click!

Ahhhh. This was more like it. Once again I was standing before a huge audience. Only this time they were on every side. Everywhere I looked they were clapping and cheering. No one had to tell me who they were cheering for. I knew. Me, the magnificent McGee. Yes, at last I'd found my place—up on stage, where all my admirers could point and clap and cheer over my greatness.

Suddenly there was the clang of a bell. The lights dimmed and . . . hold it! . . . wait a minute! I wasn't on a stage. I was—I was in a ring . . . A BOXING RING!!!

And . . . wait a minute! What wise guy stole my pants? Who put me in these . . . uh oh! Not only was I in a boxing ring, but . . . I WAS WEARING BOXING SHORTS!!!

13

The crowd gasped. Since I know my legs aren't that ugly, I figured that there was something coming up behind me. From the looks on people's faces, I could tell it was big and tall, and probably not some Girl Scout trying to sell cookies.

I took a quick look at the remote and . . . holy heart attack! I was in an HBO Sports Special!

I quickly pressed the channel selector.

PHISSST-Wop!

Nothing happened. I pressed it again.

PHISSST-Wop!

And again.

PHISSsssss . . .

Great—the batteries were dead!

Closer and closer the footsteps came. I could tell by the way the ring shook with every step that my days of painless living were quickly coming to an end. Any second now it was going to be curtains or, even worse, venetian blinds. So I did what any world-famous inventor and cartoon character would do—I screamed for the artist.

"NICHOLAS!"

Nicholas is the guy who sketches me in all of these neat adventures. Yep. That's right. All of this has just been the imaginative doodlings of my cartoonist friend, Nicholas Martin.

"NICHOLAS, GET ME OUT OF HERE! NICHO—"

Suddenly a giant boxing glove the size of the national debt grabbed me by the neck. I knew I was a goner. I knew I was history. I knew I'd never be able to watch another Brady Bunch sequel again. Then, just when things looked their worst, I saw it. . . .

Nick's famous No. 2 pencil, complete with that big

beautiful eraser, came into the scene. He quickly erased the boxer, the ring, even the audience.

"Where were you?!" I shouted angrily from the sketch pad. I was boiling mad. "I was about to get clobbered! And what about that rock video? My ears are still ringing! And that monster that kept thinking I was a cookie! Don't you have any consideration?! And another thing . . ."

I was really giving it to him. There was no shutting me up now. That is, until the No. 2 pencil came back into the scene. Then, before I could finish the sentence, it had completely erased my mouth.

I was speechless. Literally.

I began shaking my fists . . . which he also erased.

I tried jumping up and down, but my feet had also taken a hike.

Needless to say, Nick had made his point. He obviously wanted me to cool down a little. Not a bad idea. I was pretty worked up. And since I didn't have that many more portions of my body left, I decided I could chill out a little. Besides, from the looks of the adventure we were about to begin, I'd need all the cool (and body parts) I could get.

So, hang on to your hats, folks. . . .

TWO
10:07 A.M.

At precisely 10:07 Saturday morning, Nicholas and Louis threw open the front door to Nick's house and headed down his porch steps.

It was one of those great autumn mornings. The type where the air is crisp enough that you can see your breath, but not so cold that you have to wear that bulky coat your mom bought on sale. The type where the leaves are full of color, but they haven't fallen yet so your day can't be ruined by having to rake them. The type where if you just happen to have saved $150, you might go downtown to check out the new art tables. At least, that's what Nick was planning.

"You're crazy!" Louis said for about the hundredth time. (Good friends can get away with occasionally repeating themselves.) "You're gonna use that 150 bucks you've saved up for the last year and a half to buy . . . a drawing table!?"

"Well, I haven't made up my mind yet," Nick replied as they headed around the corner to their bikes. "But this isn't just any ol' drawing table."

"Yeah, right," Louis smirked. As far as he was concerned, a table was a table. I mean, what kid in his right mind would spend 150 smackaroos on some dumb old table? Not when there were more important things out there crying to be bought. Like the latest Nintendo or CD . . . or let's not forget the ever-present possibility of buying your very best friend in the whole world a portable TV for his room, which, of course, he would be willing to let you watch any time you came over.

Then there was the matter of Nick's bike. Now, it's not like it was twisted, or beat-up, or anything like that. Hey, the fact that somebody tried to buy it as a piece of modern art last week was probably just a coincidence. Just because it was always falling apart didn't mean it was worthless. I mean, all it needed was a little paint. And, well, OK, maybe some new handlebars, a new seat, an entirely new frame, a new chain, new wheels, and a couple of new tires. Other than that, it was in great shape.

"If you ask me," Louis offered, "a new bike would be a better deal."

"Hey," Nick answered as he picked up his bike and blew the rust off the handle bars. "This bike's a lean machine."

"Right," Louis chuckled. "Betcha can't even do a wheelie on that thing."

Nick turned to his friend. Was that a challenge he heard? If it was, he had a decision to make. A little decision, but a decision nonetheless. Quicker than you can say—

Hold it, hold it just a minute. . . . Did I hear the word "decision"?

What's that? Who am I? Oh, sorry. It's me again . . . McGee. And if you ask me (which you didn't, but I'll go ahead and tell you anyway 'cause that's one of the advantages of starring in your own book), this story is getting us no-where fast. If you want some real thrills and chills come on up here and join me in Central Control . . . better known as Nick's brain. Yes-siree-bob, there's no place more exciting (or frightening!) than the mind of an eleven-year-old!

Careful, watch your step. Sorry the place is such a mess, but Nick's been watching a lot of Saturday morning TV lately and it kinda trashes up the place.

All the empty shelves over to your left are where Nick will be stacking the info he gets from high school and college. The spot to the right with all these cobwebs is where he's supposed to use his logic and common sense. As you can see, the place doesn't get a lot of use.

Up ahead here, this big screen with all the knobs and switches, this is the Brain Screen Computer. From here we'll be able to see how ol' Nicky-boy makes all of his decisions. Big ones, little ones, it makes no difference. It all happens right here.

OK. Let me hop up to the terminal and type in the decision Nick has to make. What was it Louis said? Oh yeah, I've got it. . . .

CHALLENGE: "BET YOU CAN'T DO A WHEELIE."
Now, let's push a few buttons here and check out the options Nicholas has to sort through. There we go. . . .

OPTION A: "CAN I DO IT?"

Hmm, good question. Let's take a look at the screen and see. There's Nick climbing on his beat-up excuse for a bike. There's Nick trying to do a wheelie. And there's Nick flying through the air, failing with the full fury that only a full-blown failure can fail.

Well, so much for the first option. Let's check out the second. . . .

OPTION B: "WILL I BREAK MY NECK?"

My guess is, "You can count on it!" But let's check it out. Here we go again—there's Nick on his bike. There's Nick trying even harder to do a wheelie. Hey! This time he's got the front wheel up! And this time . . . well, this time he's crashing into the ground harder than a quarterback hit by a Seattle Seahawk tackle.

Okey-dokey. That takes care of Option B. And our final option . . .

OPTION C: "IF I DON'T TRY, WHAT WILL LOUIS SAY?"

Hey, check out the screen. There's ol' Louis up there. Boy, from this angle his nose looks like a giant banana! Now he's leaning toward us in a big close-up—I'm talking GIANT banana—and grinning that gigantic grin of his. Let's turn up the volume and hear what he says. . . .

"What's the matter, Nick? You chicken?"

Oh yeah, you got that right, Bub. Wanna see him lay an egg?

Well, my superior smarts are telling me this choice will be an easy one. Nick's gotta say, "No

19

*way." Any second now, that decision will pop up
on the ol' screen, and Nick will have to tell Louis
. . . oh, here it is now. See?*

DECISION: "OH WELL, I MAY AS WELL TRY."
*WHAT!!??? Nick, you don't know how to do this!
We need more data! Quick, those of you up here
with me in Central Control, strap on your safety
belts! Hurry! It's going to be a wild ride. Hang
on. . . . HANG ON. . . .*
AAAAARRRGGGGGGGHHHHHHHHH . . . !!

Back in the real world, Nicholas was trying his
best to do the wheelie. At first it didn't look like he
was going to make it. He kept pulling and pulling
and pulling. Then, with his last ounce of effort, he
finally managed to get the front wheel off the
ground.

The only problem was that it came *too* far off the
ground. And it kept coming. And coming. And coming some more. Then, before he knew it, Nick was
flying through the air. That's OK, though. It wasn't
the flying that hurt. It was the landing that
smarted—a beautiful, spread-eagle, flat-on-the-back,
knock-out-your-breath . . .
O M P H H H H ! ! !
Nick lay there, not moving, for a long moment.
"Hey," Louis called as he raced to him, "You OK?"
After a second—after the world stopped spinning
and the pain started coming—Nicholas finally
managed to let out a groan. Then, with the greatest effort, he started to get up.
"So, what say we forget the art table," Louis said

with a grin as he helped Nick to his feet. "Let's just go and find some crutches."

"Ho-ho, very funny," Nicholas mumbled as he rubbed at the pain in his backside. "Just have the ambulance drop me off at the art store."

After another moment of rear rubbing, Nick managed to get back on his bike and carefully (make that *very* carefully) start for the store. Yup, he had definitely blown that decision. Doing the wheelie was the wrong choice. But he'd learned the right lesson: showing off can be hazardous to your health—and your backside!

Speaking of sides, on the other side of town, Nick's big sister Sarah was making a decision of her own. It was Saturday, so there was only one place she could be: the mall. Just as surely as water runs downhill, as surely as little brothers are always a pain in the neck, as surely as teachers never ask the questions you study for on tests . . . if it was Saturday morning, Sarah was at the mall. It was like a tradition.

This particular day was even more than a tradition: it was a celebration! After weeks of baby-sitting and saving, Sarah finally slapped her hard-earned cash down on the counter and bought the pair of white jeans she had been eyeing for months.

These weren't just any ol' pair of white jeans. These were the primo, to-the-max, super-great-looking (complete with a sparkly handpainted rainbow) pair of white jeans.

"Wow!" Tina, her best friend, called as Sarah stepped out of the dressing room.

"Whew!" Bonnie, her second-best friend, exclaimed.

"You don't think they're too much?" Sarah asked.

"No way. Do you think they have a pair in my size?" Bonnie wondered.

Sarah threw her a look. This was pretty typical. Whenever Sarah found something that was perfect, and just for herself, Bonnie would always do her best to try to copy it. But that was Bonnie— kinda pushy, often bossy, and always, *always*, used to getting her own way. Luckily for Sarah, there wasn't a pair of the white jeans even close to Bonnie's size.

After Sarah had tried the pants on, and after her friends made the appropriate *ooohs* and *aaahs*, it didn't take much coaxing to convince her to keep wearing them. So, for the rest of the morning, no matter where they went, Sarah couldn't help feeling that everyone was watching her. She knew it probably wasn't true, but there was always the hope that she was wrong!

Now, buying things at the mall was pretty unusual for these three. Oh, they might get a slice of pizza or a taco or something like that. But most of the time they just went to hang out together and to check out all the clothes they couldn't afford. Of course, there was one other thing they always checked out. You guessed it: BOYS.

Sarah wasn't really boy-crazy, not like Tina and Bonnie. In fact, she thought the way her friends giggled and flirted with them was kind of embarrassing. Now, don't get me wrong, Sarah had plenty of friends who were boys. Most of them were pretty neat. But to think of any of them in terms of romance . . . well, Sarah figured she'd have plenty of time for that when she got older. So standing around and watching guys . . . well, that was more for the gals in romance novels and soap operas. It just wasn't for the level-headed, clear-thinking Sarah Martins of the world.

"Hey guys," Tina whispered. "Check it out. . . . Here comes my cousin Jason with one of his buddies."

Sarah and Bonnie glanced up from their tacos. Down the walkway came a couple of average-looking guys. At least Sarah thought they were average. Apparently Bonnie disagreed. The fact of the matter is, she was practically choking on a piece of lettuce. "He's gorgeous!" she whispered.

"Hey, Tina, what's happenin'?" her cousin said casually as he and his friend sauntered up.

"Hi, Jas. Not much," Tina answered.

"Who are your friends?" Jason asked. He said "friends," but by the way he was checking out Sarah it was pretty obvious he meant "friend." Sarah glanced down. She could feel her cheeks start to burn. Part of her was pleased with the attention, but part of her was also uncomfortable.

"This here's Bonnie," Tina said.

"Hi!" Bonnie croaked, still trying to swallow her lettuce.

"And Sarah," Tina added.

Sarah smiled.

Jason stared. That is, until his friend gave him a jab in the gut. "Oh, uh, and this here's uh . . . uh . . . Willard."

An uneasy silence settled over the group. But since Tina could never survive over eight and a half seconds of silence, she tried something else. "Jason here, he races stock cars . . . don't you, Jas?"

"Yeah, that's right," he grinned. "Got a big race tonight. You babes oughta come by and check it out."

"We'd love to!" Bonnie chirped in delight.

Tina gave her a look that would freeze the sun. A look that said, "I know it's probably not possible, but could you maybe play it just a little bit cool?"

Jason didn't notice. He was still staring at Sarah. "Decent jeans," was all he said.

Sarah's face got hotter.

Then, turning to the rest of the group he finished, "Maybe we'll see you there." With that he gave Tina a little punch in the arm and headed off. "Take care, Cuz. . . ."

"You, too, Jas," Tina said, looking very pleased with herself. The guys were less than five feet away when the girls quickly pulled into a little circle of whispers, giggles, and laughter.

"He really likes you," Tina crowed.

"You think so?" Bonnie asked as she straightened her hair.

"Not you . . . I meant Sarah."

Sarah grinned. Now that Jason wasn't right

there staring away at her, being liked suddenly felt a lot better.

"And the pants," Bonnie admitted. "He loved the pants!"

"So are you going?" Tina demanded.

"Where?" Sarah asked.

"To the races, dork-brain."

"How? I don't have any way to get—"

"No sweat," Tina interrupted. "I can get my dad to drop us off."

"I don't know . . . ," Sarah stalled.

"C'mon, it'll be great!" Bonnie added.

"How do you know your mom will let you go?" Sarah asked Bonnie.

"She's just like Tina's dad—she'll let me do anything I want," Bonnie said with confidence.

"Jason really likes you, I can tell," Tina said, giving Sarah a knowing nod. "Hey, maybe he can get us a pit pass . . . that's where the real action is during the race."

"Cool!" Bonnie exclaimed.

Sarah didn't say much. She wasn't so sure it was all that "cool." I mean, Jason was sixteen, maybe older. What would she, a little fourteen-year-old, be doing hanging around some old guy like that? Besides, what would her folks say? Oh, sure, it wasn't like an official date, or anything like that. It was just some girls going to the stock car races. Lots of kids did that. Still . . .

Sarah's thoughts began to churn. She knew she'd have to make a decision. She just wasn't too sure what that decision would be.

THREE
10:42 A.M.

Nicholas thought The Art Shop was a pretty cool place. He was hoping Louis would think so, too. But the look on Louis's face when they entered the store told Nick his hopes were too high. Impressing Louis was tough. I mean, for Louis to think something was "cool," it would have to be extra-ultra-totally-super-cool-to-the-max for the rest of us mortals. It wasn't that Louis was hard to please—he was just the only kid Nick knew who had come back from California totally bored. I mean, Louis's idea of a time without boredom would be something like a ride on the space shuttle . . . and then only if they had a big-screen TV and an excellent stereo system.

Nick sighed and looked around the store. Off in the corner, by itself, was the art table he had been talking about. As he had pointed out, this wasn't just any old art table. It was definitely the Super-Deluxe-with-Everything-You-Need-and-Then-Some

Model. This puppy was so high-tech it looked like it came right off the Starship Enterprise.

Nick slowly walked toward it. He gently rubbed his hand over the chrome-and-glass borders. In awe he touched the sleek pen and pencil tray. Next, he tried out the ultra-high-tech lamp. Even the art file drawer looked like something Mr. Sulu should be using to "lock on coordinates."

He turned to Louis with a look of triumph. He didn't have to say a word. It should be obvious that this was no ordinary table. Any minute now Louis would be apologizing for all the putdowns he'd made about the cost of the table. Any minute now he'd nod his head saying, "You're right, Nick, this table is awesome." Any minute now . . .

"150 bucks?!" Louis crowed. "Does this thing do your homework, too?"

Nicholas closed his eyes. Sometimes he hated reality. But before he had a chance to respond to Louis, an answer came from around the corner.

"Not quite," a cheery voice remarked. "But it does get over twenty-five miles per gallon."

The kids looked up just as Graham Boatwright, the store owner, joined them. He was a jolly, well-fed fellow. It wouldn't be fair to say he's fat, but there was no mistaking the fact that he hadn't missed a meal in a while . . . quite a while. Come to think of it, he didn't miss too many in-between-meal meals, either.

"Hi, Graham," Nick said with a grin.

"What d'ya say, Nick?" Graham asked as he ran his hand over the sleek surface. "Ain't she a beaut?"

Nick had to nod.

"'Course I can't guarantee it'll make you draw any better."

"I know," Nick agreed. "But maybe using a table like this would, you know . . . inspire me."

"Hey, c'mon. That's what sunsets are for."

The two exchanged smiles.

Louis started looking around. It's not like he was bored or anything like that. But if they happened to catch some action, like getting hit by a good earthquake or hurricane right now, you wouldn't hear him complaining.

"I know what you mean about inspiration," Graham continued. "In art school they used to tell us, 'You're only as good as your tools.'"

"Really?" Nick asked. "So what did you do?"

"I went out and bought a new wrench and socket set!"

The two broke out laughing.

Louis figured this was artist-type humor, 'cause it sure didn't do anything for him. The best he could do was roll his eyes.

"OK . . . ," Graham chuckled. "Enough comedy."

"So that's what it was," Louis muttered.

Fortunately Graham didn't hear him. "Now, back to the sales pitch. What do your parents think?"

"Well . . . ," Nick hesitated. "I don't think they're against it, but I'm not really sure they know all the details."

"Like maybe you're nuts!" Louis cracked.

Graham gave a little smile. He found Louis's humor about as funny as Louis found his. "Look," he said turning back to Nick. "Why not have one final sit-down and talk it over with your folks." Then he added with a grin, "Have you tried holding your breath till they agree to pay for half?"

Nick chuckled. "No . . . the last time Jamie, my little sister, tried that, my dad said she looked better in purple."

Again, the two guys laughed. Louis barely heard them. He was busy hoping that the rumble of that passing truck outside was a jet liner coming in for a crash landing. Maybe that would liven up the party.

No such luck.

"Well," Graham finally finished. "I don't want to

rush you, but this is the last one I've got in stock. I'm afraid you're going to have to make up your mind pretty soon."

Nick nodded. It was a tough decision, no doubt about it. And he didn't have much time to make it. But right now it was time for another decision. One for which Louis would be eternally grateful. . . .

It was time to leave the art store.

Meanwhile, on the drive home from the mall, Tina was forcing someone else to make a decision.

"Daddy?" Tina's voice had a smooth, slow drawl to it.

Sarah turned from the car window to look at her friend. She knew Tina had come from the South. But she'd never heard her use this thick an accent before.

"What's up, Sugar?" her father asked. Tina's mother was supposed to have picked them up. But since her dad was in the area he had decided to swing on by.

"Well, me an' the girls here . . . " Tina curled up closer to her father. "We was kinda hopin' ta watch Jason do some racin' at the stock car rally to-night."

Sarah watched with interest. With every word Tina's voice seemed to get warmer and softer. The girl was really pouring it on. In fact, if her voice got any sweeter she was going to give everyone in the car a toothache. But her father didn't seem to notice.

"An' we was wonderin' if you'd like ta take little

ol' me an' my friends over there later on." By now she was actually resting her head on his shoulder.

"Oh, I'm sorry, darlin'," he answered. And you could tell by the tone in his voice that he really was. "But I promised ta take Jimmy an' his friends ta the cinema."

"Well, that just figures," Tina scorned. Suddenly her warm southern voice had an icy northern chill.

Sarah continued to watch. She had heard that Tina could get anything she wanted from her folks. Now, for the first time, she had the chance to watch the "expert" in action.

But nothing happened. In fact, for several moments they just rode in silence. What was wrong? Had Tina given up—just like that? Sarah continued to watch. Then she saw it. Tina's dad was starting to fidget. Soon, he was actually beginning to throw nervous glances in his daughter's direction.

Tina said nothing.

He cleared his throat.

She still said nothing. By now it was becoming obvious that Tina was giving her dad the silent treatment. And it was pretty obvious it was starting to do the trick.

"I hope ya undastand, Cupcake," Tina's dad said apologetically.

"I 'undastand' plenty," Tina scowled as she folded her arms and looked out the window.

"Now, Darlin', what's that supposed ta mean?"

"It just means that whenever Jimmie wants to go somewhere he goes. But I ask fer one litta favor, an' ya'd a thought I'd asked fer the moon."

"Now, Honey, ya know that ain't so."

"Is too."

"Sugar—"

"Is too, an' you know it!"

Sarah caught her breath. If she talked back to her dad like that she'd be lucky to get out of the house for a year. But not Tina. She had her father exactly where she wanted him.

"Listen . . . I have an idea," he said. "What say I swing by an' get us all some pizza. Maybe yer friends can stay over an'—"

"No, thank ya. I am not interested," Tina said coldly.

Sarah marveled. Tina's father was making peace offerings, but the girl would have none of it. She was obviously holding out for a higher offer. Yes sir, she was a pro. No doubt about it.

More silence.

Again Tina's father shifted uncomfortably. If there was one thing he didn't like it was not being liked . . . especially by his *"darlin'"* *daughter.*

"Sugar?"

More silence.

"Sugar, come on now an' talk ta me."

Still more silence.

Then it finally happened. He broke. The poor man just could not bear being shut out. "Well, what say we try this," he offered. "Why don't I drop you an' yer little friends off at tha races then go on over an' take Jimmy to the cinema. How's that sound?"

"I'm afraid it'd jus' be too much trouble for ya," Tina answered, her voice still stiff and cool.

Again Sarah smiled. This girl knew all the tricks.

"No," her father insisted. "It wouldn't be that much trouble. It would work out jus' fine that-a-way."

"I jus' don't know. . . ."

Boy, talk about playing hard to get! The amazing thing was, it was working.

"Please, Darlin', it would be my pleasure."

"Well. . . ." Tina pretended to hesitate. Her dad was definitely feeling the pressure. Finally, in desperation, he had one last thought. The thought Tina had been waiting for him to come up with all along.

"Tell ya what," he said triumphantly. "If you let me take ya, I bet I'd even be willin' ta pay fer yer admission. What da ya say ta that?"

"Would ya?" Once again Tina's voice was getting that southern warmth to it. "Would ya really?"

"Of course," he said, "And fer all your friends, too." He broke into a confident smile. Boy howdy, nobody could say he didn't know how to handle his little girl. Yep, he was a reg'lar child-rearin' genius.

"Oh, thank ya, Daddy," Tina said, beaming.

"Well, I reckon it's the least I can do, don't you?"

"Oh, Daddy," she said as she curled up next to him again. "You're so good ta me."

"I know, darlin' girl," he said, putting his arm around her. "But I jus' wouldn't have it any other way."

Sarah looked on, her mouth hanging open. Tina glanced up and gave her a little wink. Yes sir, everything had worked out exactly as she had planned.

Outside the art store, Louis and Nick were getting on their bikes. Suddenly Louis had a brainstorm.

34

"Hey, I know just what you need to relax the ol' brain cells. Let's go over to Riley's Arcade and zap some aliens!"

Nick glanced over to his friend. It was true, unwinding with some video games might help him relax and make up his mind. But if he decided to do that, it would—

Now hold it, hold it just a minute! Did my ever-so-perfect hearing hear the word it thought it heard? Did somebody decide it was time to decide another decision?

Well, come on down . . . er, up, or wherever this Brain Screen thing is, and let's take a look at ol' Nicky-boy's thoughts.

First, let me type in the question.

QUESTION: "SHOULD I PLAY VIDEO GAMES?"
Now for the options. . . .

OPTION A: "IS THIS GOOD FOR ME?"
Hmmm. Let's see what comes up on the screen. Hey, there's the video arcade. Oh, and here's Nick at the "Trash the Mutant Blood-Sucking Pigs from Venus" game. It's his favorite. Uh oh, wait a minute. Take a look at those eyes. He must have been here all afternoon. And that frizzled hair. Looks like he's been going to Albert Einstein's barber. Talk about bushed. I mean, if this guy was any more burned-out, he'd be a pile of ashes.

Oh, look, here comes good ol' Louis. Look at that, he's got the same beat-up expression. Hold on, he's about to say something important. . . .

"Got any more quarters?"

Boy, talk about the living dead. The guy sounds like he's half-asleep.

"I'm flat broke."

That was Nicholas—and he is asleep.

Well, that takes care of Option A. The arcade is about as good for Nick as going skinny-dipping in the middle of December . . . in Alaska . . . under the ice. OK, so let's see what's next on the list.

OPTION B: "WHAT DO MY FOLKS SAY?"

And up on the screen we see . . . oh, it's Mom. She's pointing to a watch that's strapped to her wrist that's the size of Roseanne Barr's mouth. What's she saying?

"Remember, be home by noon."

Let's see. It's fifteen minutes to noon now, and it takes fifteen minutes to get home. Hmmm . . . Looks like it's time to get out the old calculator. Ah, here we go. Now, we just add the seven, carry the three, find the square root of 3.14, divide that by its common denominator, multiply it by $E=MC^2$, throw in a pinch of salt and two cloves of garlic, click your heels together three times, and we get . . .

Well, I'm not sure what we get. (Math was never one of my strong suits.) But whatever we get, it's a safe guess those Blood-Sucking Pigs from Venus are safe for another day.

All rightee, and our last option in the old process:

OPTION C: "WHAT DOES THE WISE MAN SAY?"

The Wise Man, huh? I wonder who . . . ? Hey, will you take a look at that? Here comes some old gee-

zer in robes and a long, flowing beard. Look at all those books he's carrying. This guy must really be wise, I mean, to be readin' all of those books. Either that, or he's heading up some paper drive. Hold it. He's pointing to a book on his lap. What's he saying?

"The Scripture says, 'Honor your father and mother.'"

No argument there, Grandpa. But wait a sec. Doesn't this guy look kinda suspicious? Those eyes . . . that mouth. I mean, if it wasn't for the beard, he'd look like—Hold the phone, Fred! He's pullin' down the beard. It's a fake!

That's . . . that's Nick's dad under there!! Now it looks like he wants to say something else. Let's see if he has any other precious pearls of wisdom to share. . . .

"Nicholas! Did you mow the lawn yet?"

Now, that's more like it. Yes-siree, disguise 'em all you want, but no matter what you do, dads just can't stop being dads.

So where was I? Oh yeah. Let's press the ol' button here and get Nick's final decision.

There he is, back in front of the art shop. Let's listen to his conclusion:

"No way, Louis. An hour in there and I won't have enough money to buy a pencil, much less an art table. Besides, I'm supposed to be home by noon."

Well, what do you know. He got one right. Nice work, Nick.

There they go, hopping on their bikes and merrily pedaling down the street.

Ahhh . . . I just love happy endings, don't you?

FOUR
11:59 A.M.

It was exactly 11:59 A.M. Not only had Nicholas made it home on time, but he actually had a minute to spare! Imagine being home early! What a concept! If he kept that up, he'd be giving the rest of kidhood a bad name!

He plopped down at the table just in time to see the old standby lunch (tomato soup and a grilled cheese sandwich) shoved under his face. Luckily, he managed to grab a handful of chips before they disappeared forever into the "Forbidden Zone"— better known as Sarah's side of the table.

Sarah wasn't saying much. She never did. That is unless she had a juicy putdown, wisecrack, or complaint—which, come to think of it, happened to be most of the time. But that should go without saying. After all, she *was* the older sister. I mean, she did have her end of the relationship to keep up.

Today, though, she said nothing. Maybe she was trying to be polite. Or maybe she finally realized it was time to start treating Nick with some respect. Yeah, well, I wouldn't bet on it. Actually, Sarah's silence had nothing to do with Nick. It had a lot to do with the fight she had just had with Mom. . . .

"But why can't I go?" she had asked.

"Sarah," her mother had sighed for the hundredth time. "You're only fourteen and—"

"Almost fifteen," Sarah had interrupted. "I'm closer to fifteen than fourteen."

"Fine. The point is we agreed that you wouldn't start dating until you were—"

"But this isn't a date! I'm just going to the stock car races with Tina."

"To see some older boy we haven't even met!" Mom had felt her voice getting a little sharp. She hated it when that happened, yet, somehow, Sarah always knew how to get it to happen.

"But I'm not going to see *him*." Sarah had insisted. "He's just getting us some pit passes so we can go down into—"

"You're going into the pit area!?"

"Well, yeah. Tina says that's where all the action—"

"That's where all the cars zoom in and out!"

Sarah stared at the table and bit her lip. She'd blown it, no doubt. With one slip of the tongue she had cut off all possibility of going. Now, not only was Mom thinking she had a serious case on some older grease monkey, she was also picturing Sarah standing in the middle of some racetrack dodging cars all night.

It was useless. Sarah knew it. Still, she had one weapon left. A weapon she'd seen Tina use on her dad with the greatest of success. Now it was Sarah's turn to try it. . . .

Sarah sulked. She would not say another word.

For a beginner, she did a pretty good job of it. That is, until Nick barged in and brought up the topic of the art table. Then . . . well, it was like she couldn't help herself. It was like her older-sister genes suddenly took over.

"Have you considered investing in something really worthwhile?" she snapped. "Like clothes?"

Now it's true, she had a point. I mean, Nick's idea of fashion was throwing on the first things he grabbed in the morning. It made little difference what color they were, or even if they matched. If they were the first things his hand fumbled for, they were the first things he wore.

"Cholfes?" Nick mumbled through a mouthful of grilled cheese sandwich. "I mont to be an artist, mot a model."

"No danger in that," Sarah agreed.

"You look fine," Mom said as she handed him a glass of milk. It wasn't really the truth. But, after all, moms are expected to say that sort of thing. It's in their contract.

"Thanks," Nick answered. "So when can I talk to you and Dad about the art table? There's only one left and I gotta make a decision by Monday."

"Your father ought to be home soon. Let's talk it over after dinner." Suddenly a thought came to her mind. A thought that only a motherly mind can think. If Nick had been paying attention he would have seen it coming. He would have been able to make his escape ahead of time. But it was too late now.

"Hey," she asked. "Speaking of Monday, don't you have a book report due?"

Nick was trapped. "Well, yeah," he said as he picked up his sandwich and started for the family room. Maybe he could still get away. "I'm almost done. I'll finish it right after Sci-Fi Theat—"

He never finished the sentence. Mom knew exactly what he was getting at and exactly how to put a stop to it. "No way," she insisted. "You were at the art store all morning. With church tomorrow you won't have time."

"Oh, Mom. . . ." But Nick knew there was no changing her mind.

"Finish the report and then we'll see about Sci-Fi Theater," she said as she put the milk back in the fridge. "But I really doubt you'll have time to—" She looked back toward him and came to a stop.

Nick had already taken off for his room. There wasn't much time. But if there was any way of getting that book read before seeing Sci-Fi Theater . . . he'd do it.

Mom couldn't help breaking into a smile. Well, there was one thing you could say about Nick—he was determined. She looked over at Sarah, who was once again chewing her sandwich in silence. Of course, you could say the same thing about Sarah, too. . . .

Up in his room, Nick was plowing though *Treasure Island*. He was reading the sentences as fast as his little eyeballs could move. Of course, he didn't know half of what he was reading, but at least he was reading.

Suddenly a sickening thought came to his mind. He reached for the back of the book and started flipping the pages.

"Oh, great," he sighed. "I've still got two more chapters to read. This will take forever. Unless . . ." You could see the wheels starting to turn in his mind. "Unless I just read the last couple of pages and—"

Uh-oh . . . Here we go again. Time for Nicholas to make another decision. But this time it's a little more tricky. Not only does it deal with using bad judgment, like the daredevil wheelie, but it is a question of choosing between right and wrong. Let's type in the question and take a look at the data.

QUESTION: "SHOULD I GIVE A REPORT ON A BOOK I HAVEN'T FINISHED READING?"
The options to consider:

OPTION A: "IS IT RIGHT?"
And up on the screen we have . . . Oh, it's our favorite blue-eyed bully, Derrick Cryder. My, my, he looks especially frightening today, dressed in his favorite leather coat and brass knuckles. Looks like he'll be convincing a few more munchkins that they won't be needing their lunch money. Wait a minute, he's about to say something to Nick. Let's listen and see what cunning words our conniving con has to convey.

"Look stupid, everybody does it. Man, I just read the inside cover."

Well, thanks for sharing, Derrick. At least we have our answer about right or wrong. Now on to . . .

OPTION B: "WHAT WOULD THE OTHER KIDS SAY IF THEY FOUND OUT?"

Hey, there's Renee and Louis with Nicholas up on the screen. Gee, they don't look so hot. What's the matter? They got the flu? Renee's doing the talking (so, what else is new?). Let's listen. . . .

"Gee, Nick. We thought you were different when it came to being honest and stuff."

Not good, Nicky-roo. Not good at all. So let's go on to the next option. . . .

OPTION C: "WHY DO I WANT TO DO THIS?"

And here we have Nick sitting in front of the ol' tube. Let's take a peek at what he's watching.

Oh great, it's one of those Japanese sci-fi flicks. You know the type . . . with all those fakey monsters strolling through fakey models that are supposed to be real buildings. Then, of course, there's the cornball music. And let's not forget the scream ing—there has to be lots and lots of screaming . . . and it must never match the the actors' lip movements.

There he is now. There's your average run-of-the-mill monster rising out of your average run-of-the-mill ocean about to attack your average run-of-the-mill city.

Now he's knocking over buildings, swatting down toy planes, trouncing on Match Box cars, and flossing his teeth with those ever-popular sparking power lines.

Yes-siree-bob. I tell you, Nick, this stuff is really classic. The type of thing I'd love to be cheating on book reports and ruining my reputation over.

Well, enough of that. Let's take a look at our final option. . . .

OPTION D: "WHAT DOES THE WISE MAN SAY?"

Ah, yes, and there's . . . wait a minute, it's dorkey Derrick again. Hey, I said wise "man" not wise "guy." Here, let me just give this screen a little kick like they taught us in computer repair school. . . .

K-THWACK!

There, that's better. Now we have the old geezer (alias Dad) speaking again.

"And the Scriptures say, 'Give me understanding that I may obey your law. . . .' "

Ah, yes, "obedience." Not always a popular word, but definitely one worth keeping around.

Well, now that we've got all of our data, let's press the old decision button here and see what comes up.

DECISION: "I WANTED TO READ THE WHOLE BOOK ANYWAY."

Atta boy, Nicholas! I knew you could do it! You're 2-for-3 in the decision department! But hang on! It's going to start getting crazy. . . .

44

FIVE
6:30 P.M.

It was Saturday night and Sarah had just hung up the phone. She wasn't sure why or how it had happened—but somehow Tina had managed to convince her to go to the races.

"It will be perfectly safe," Tina had said. "Daddy will be with the three of us the whole time."

"Yeah, but . . ."

"Besides, it's time they quit treating you like a little girl. I mean, you're practically fifteen. Almost a woman."

"Yeah, but . . ."

"Just tell them you're going over to my—no, you better make that Bonnie's house. Just tell them you're going to Bonnie's. . . ."

"Yeah, but . . ."

"It won't be a lie. I mean, you *will* be going there first. It won't be your fault that Daddy and I just happen to swing by and ask you to come along."

No doubt about it, Tina had a devious mind. And she wasn't afraid to use that mind on Sarah. Over

and over again she had argued and reasoned . . .
until Sarah finally had crumbled. *Really,* she
thought as she hung up the phone, *I had no
choice. I had to say yes.* Either that or, as Tina so
clearly pointed out, "You'll just be a total loser for
the rest of your life."

But if everything Tina had said was so logical
and made such perfect sense, how come Sarah felt
so bad? I mean, she barely had the receiver back
in its cradle before the waves of guilt began to
wash over her.

Still, she had made her decision. Now all she
had to do was live with it.

Meanwhile, over in the family room, Nick was still
working on his decision. "It's really neat," he was
saying to his folks. "I mean, it's got an art file
drawer attached to keep my McGee drawings and
stuff . . . and a tray for pencils . . . and it looks
great . . . and—and . . ."

Suddenly Nicholas came to a stop. If it was such
a great deal, how come he was working so hard to
convince his parents? Maybe it really wasn't his
parents he was trying to convince. Maybe he was
still trying to convince himself.

"It sounds wonderful, Son," Dad finally offered.

"But, Honey . . . " It was Mom. Just as he'd always be "Son" to his dad, he'd always be "Honey"
to his mom. "Honey," she continued, "what's
wrong with your old art table?"

"Well . . ." Nick's mind was searching desperately.
"It's old! I mean, I've had it ever since . . . ever since
I was a kid."

46

There was no missing the brief smiles that appeared on his parents' lips.

At last Dad cleared his throat and got very serious. There was no mistaking it, the verdict was about to be handed down. "Son . . . we know you've saved this money for a long time."

You're right about that. But what about the decision?

Dad continued. "You worked for it . . . you earned it . . . and . . . "

Yeah, yeah, go on, go on.

"And if you're certain you want to spend it on a new art table . . . "

Nick held his breath.

"Well, that's OK with us."

ALL RIGHT! HE SCORES! A BIG T.D. FOR THE KID!

Well, at least that's what Nick figured he should have thought. But something was wrong. Even with his parents' permission, something still wasn't right.

Mom was the first to notice. "So, what's the problem, Honey?"

"I don't know . . . I thought if you guys said OK, that would be it. But . . . " he hesitated for a second. "I still don't really know what to do."

Mom and Dad exchanged glances. Finally Dad spoke.

"I know how you feel, Nick. And I think you're using the right approach. I mean, it seems like you've given this decision a lot of thought, and you've come to us for advice. That's great. But there's still one thing left you have to do."

"What's that?" Nick asked.

"Pray."

Nicholas looked at his father. As usual, the man was right on the button. Coming to his parents for advice was good, but now they were turning the decision back to him. Now *he'd* have to make it. And if he really wanted to make the right decision, he'd have to get one other opinion: God's.

Nick sighed. Turning to Mom and Dad for a quick yes or no was an easy solution—sometimes too easy. But turning to the Lord and asking for his wisdom . . . well, that was a little different. It wasn't necessarily harder, but it was different. And it was a difference he'd have to get used to the older he got. . . .

Try as she might Sarah couldn't get rid of the knot growing in her stomach. It was there when she asked Mom if she could go to Bonnie's house. (She half wished Mom would say no, but she didn't.)

It was a little bigger as she put on her new white jeans, threw on a coat, and headed out the front door.

It was a lot bigger when Tina and her dad arrived at Bonnie's to pick them up.

And it was about the size of a watermelon as they rode in the station wagon toward the races. The fact that Tina's little brother and all his friends were bouncing up and down on the seats and throwing Gummi Bears at each other didn't

help much. The fact that Tina had the radio cranked up full volume helped even less.

"You girls have a good time!" her dad hollered as they pulled into the parking lot.

"Yes, Daddy," Tina shouted.

"You bet," Bonnie yelled.

Sarah didn't answer. She figured no one could hear her from the back seat anyway.

By now the car had stopped and the girls were piling out. Sarah noticed something green and gooey sticking to her new white jeans—a lime Gummi Bear (half-chewed, of course) had found a permanent home on her right leg. *Oh great*, she thought as she bent over and started picking it off.

"The movie gets out at 9:30," Tina's dad yelled as he began pulling away. "We'll be by ta pick ya up 'bout a quarter ta ten."

"Thank ya, Daddy!" Tina called.

He gave a wave and was gone.

Suddenly Sarah looked up. "Wait a minute. . . . Wait a minute! Where's your dad going?"

"Taking my brother and his scum-bucket friends to the movies."

"But . . . didn't you say he'd be with us?" Sarah tried to be cool, but there was no missing the concern in her voice.

"Did I?" Tina asked innocently. "Oh, well, he'll be back in a couple of hours."

Sarah wasn't thrilled, and she made no effort to hide it.

"Come on," Bonnie chided, "don't be such a prude. It's only a couple of hours. What trouble can we get into in just two hours?"

"Oh, I bet we'll find something," Tina giggled.

"Let's hope so," Bonnie giggled back. "Come on, let's go!"

"But guys . . . ," Sarah called. "Guys!"

It did no good. Her two friends were already half-way across the parking lot. Not wanting to be left alone, Sarah let out a sigh and followed them . . . all the time, of course, picking at the gooey green gunk stuck to her leg.

Back at home, Nicholas was up in his room. He wasn't reading. He wasn't inventing one of his neat inventions. He wasn't even drawing a McGee adventure.

He was making out a list. A decision list. On one side were all of the reasons to buy the art table. On the other side were all of the reasons not to buy. But things weren't going the way he'd hoped. It seemed he had more than enough reasons for the "Not to Buy" column and only a couple for the "Buy" column. He tried to even them out, but pretty soon the whole thing was looking a little lopsided:

DECISION LIST

Reasons to Buy	Reasons NOT to Buy
It would keep me organized.	It costs too much.
It would be fun.	Could buy lots of other things.
It would be fun.	Keep saving for new bike.
It would be fun.	Don't really need it.
It would be fun.	Use money to help others.
It would be fun.	Save for college.

After a moment, Nick crumpled the paper and tossed it into the trash. This definitely was not going the way he wanted.

"Isn't this great?"

"WHAT?"

"I SAID, ISN'T THIS GREAT!"

The roar of the stock cars was too loud. Sarah had to read Bonnie's lips to figure out what she was saying.

"YES," Sarah finally shouted back. "BUT ARE YOU SURE WE'RE SUPPOSED TO BE HERE??"

"WHAT?" Bonnie shouted.

"WE'RE NOT SIXTEEN—THE SIGN SAID YOU HAVE TO BE SIXTEEN TO BE IN THE PITS!"

"WE GOT THE PASSES, DIDN'T WE?"

"YEAH, BUT—"

"WHAT??"

Sarah just shook her head. She'd been called a prude once tonight. Once was enough. If they weren't supposed to be there, well, let Tina's cousin, Jason, get in trouble. After all, he was the one who got them the passes.

To be honest, Sarah was a little disappointed in Jason's reaction when he saw her. She wasn't expecting him to do handsprings. But she was expecting more than a quick "Hi" before he began yelling at his partner to fix the distributor or carburetor or whatever it was.

Obviously he didn't know what she had gone through to get there—the lying, the sneaking, the knot in her gut . . . and now the permanent loss of hearing.

52

But that was half an hour ago. Now Jason was out on the track with half a dozen other cars. Now they were all fighting for position as they waited for the starting flag, and the beginning of the race.

Tina and Bonnie were practically glowing with excitment. I mean, here they were, right in the heart of the action. Everywhere they looked, people were running, sweating, swearing, smelling of gas, borrowing tools, desperately trying to fix their cars for their upcoming heats. And here they were, three kids, standing right in the middle of it.

"There they go!" Tina shouted.

All heads turned back to the track just in time to watch the cars get the green flag and start the race.

Suddenly everyone was going full throttle . . . fighting for position . . . gunning . . . braking . . . trying to squeeze past one another. Anything went—and that's what they tried: anything.

The noise was deafening. The smell of exhaust was suffocating.

Around and around the track they roared, always staying in a tight pack. Each time they thundered past the pit, the girls could feel the wind from the cars against their faces.

And then it happened. . . .

The second-place car, a yellow one, made its move and somehow forced the lead car against the wall. The car didn't hit the wall hard, just hard enough to lose a wheel . . . which bounced out into the middle of the track! A green car hit the tire and began spinning, which sent a red car sliding . . . and careening right into Jason's front side!

53

"Oh, my gosh!" Tina screamed.

"He's been hit!" Bonnie cried.

The three girls watched in horror as Jason fought for control. First he swerved to the right, then to the left. Somehow he managed to hang on until, at last, he spun out into the pit area. There was dust and smoke everywhere. And most of the smoke was coming from Jason's car!

"Looks like a fire!" somebody yelled. Immediately half a dozen men raced toward the car—many with fire extinguishers.

"Jason! Jason!!" Tina screamed as she started running toward his car. It was more than five-hundred feet away and already surrounded by people, but there was no stopping her.

"Tina!" Bonnie shouted. "Tina, come back!!" She started after her friend. Sarah also shouted and was about to follow. But then she saw it. . . .

The green car, which had spun out, was now bouncing into the pit area.

And heading right for Bonnie!

"Bonnie, look out!" Sarah shouted. But no one heard.

Suddenly, everything became a slow-motion movie. . . .

The car swerved hard to the right to try to miss Bonnie. Catching the movement out of the corner of her eye, Bonnie turned to see the car. The front end had managed to miss her, but the rear end was sliding directly toward her. She opened her mouth to scream, but she didn't have time. She tried to jump out of the way, but she was too late.

Sarah felt paralyzed as she watched the rear fender catch Bonnie on the leg, and send her flying through the air.

"BONNIE!" Even Sarah's scream sounded as if it was in slow motion as she watched her friend sail through the air. Finally Bonnie hit the ground— hard . . . too hard.

Sarah tore after her, her feet flying across the ground.

"BONNIE!" But no one heard. No one saw. Everybody was still paying attention to Jason—pulling him out of his smoking car—putting out the fire in his engine. "BONNIE!!"

Bonnie wasn't answering. She wasn't raising her head and looking around with that silly grin she always wore when she did something stupid. She wasn't moving . . . at all. She just lay on the ground like some limp, broken doll.

Sarah reached her friend and dropped to her knees. The ground was soaked in water and oil. She could feel the cold dampness as it soaked through her pants.

"Bonnie . . . Bonnie . . ." Sarah said in a trembling voice. But there was no answer. Sarah scooped her hands under Bonnie's head, and felt something wet and sticky on her fingers. Blood. Bonnie was bleeding. Not a lot, but enough.

"Somebody help us!" Sarah cried. "Somebody please help us!"

The driver of the green car had leaped out and was racing toward them. Now other people had noticed and were starting to follow.

Sarah was cradling Bonnie's bleeding head on

her lap. She was rocking her, ever so slightly, back and forth, back and forth . . . and she was sobbing.

"Somebody help us!" Her voice was so choked the words came out in a whisper. The tears were flowing and they wouldn't stop. "Somebody . . . please help us. . . ."

SIX
10:30 P.M.

Sarah sat in the hospital waiting room. She didn't
know how long she'd been there, but if it had been
a couple of minutes past forever she wouldn't have
been surprised.

Back at the racetrack it had been a nightmare:
people running, the ambulance zooming up, paramedics shouting orders. All of this as the driver of
the green car kept yelling, "I didn't see her . . . I
just didn't see her!"

The paramedics had moved in and gently pried
Sarah away from Bonnie. At first Sarah wouldn't
let go, but their calm coaxing finally had con-
vinced her there was nothing more she could do.
After all, they were the experts. It was up to them
now.

Before Sarah knew it, she had been eased back
into the group of spectators. Suddenly she was
just part of the crowd, jostling and craning her
neck like all the others just to get a peek at what
was happening to her friend.

She hadn't been able to see much. Being five-foot-two had its disadvantages. She had only caught occasional glimpses of the paramedics hovering over Bonnie. It had looked like they had attached some sort of tubing to her arm. Then they'd turned around and pulled a collapsible gurney out of the ambulance.

Sarah had gotten another glance of them carefully slipping a board under Bonnie and strapping her to it. Then, in one quick movement, they had hoisted her up, laid her on the gurney, and wheeled her toward the ambulance.

Sarah remembered how the flashing red and orange lights had hurt her eyes—but she'd continued to watch. The first attendant had hopped inside with Bonnie, while the other slammed the doors and raced around to the front.

Then they were off. Just like that. Just like that, her friend was gone. Just like that, she felt all alone and deserted. But there was one thing that made her feel a little better. Not enough to smile, but enough to ease the pain . . . a little.

As they were wheeling Bonnie toward the ambulance Sarah caught a glimpse of her face. Her eyes were open. They were scared, looking all around, and filled with tears. But at least they were open.

That had been almost an hour and a half ago. Since then, Tina's dad had picked them up and they were all waiting in the hospital. Tina, her dad, Jason, Bonnie's mom, the driver of the green car, and Sarah.

But two more people were about to arrive.

Sarah's parents suddenly appeared in the doorway. They were not smiling.

"Mom! Dad!" Sarah was up on her feet and in Mom's arms before she knew it. She buried her face deep into Mom's coat. She hadn't done that since she was a kid but she was doing it now. It was like she wanted to stay buried in there forever—never wanting to leave that comfort and safety again.

She wasn't sure why, but she was crying . . . sobbing. And to be honest, Mom was fighting back tears of her own.

"Sweetheart, are you all right?" Dad asked her, his voice a little unsteady. But she couldn't answer—she was still sobbing into Mom's coat. "Sweetheart?" he repeated, his voice growing more concerned. "Sweetheart?"

At last Sarah was able to look up. "Oh, Daddy. . . ," she sobbed, then she threw her arms around him.

"Honey," Mom said, brushing away her own tears. "We were so worried . . . it could have been you who was hurt."

All Sarah could do was nod as she hung on to both of them. The teenager in her knew she should be embarrassed acting this way in public, in front of Tina and Jason and everyone. But right now she didn't care. Right now she wanted to keep holding on to them and never let go.

Mom and Dad exchanged glances. They had been pretty angry when they got the phone call—when they learned that Sarah had disobeyed and deceived them. All the way over in the car, Dad kept saying how upset and disappointed he was . . . and what type of discipline Sarah would have to face.

Right now, though, wasn't a time for discipline. He knew that. It was a time for love. Oh, make no mistake about it—the discipline would come and it would come hard. But right now it was time to hold, and hug, and even cry a little.

A few minutes later, the doctor entered. Suddenly everything got very quiet.

"Mrs. Putnam?" he said, looking at the group gathered there.

"Yes," Bonnie's mom said, as she nervously stepped forward. Sarah's folks stood right beside her in case the news was bad.

"Your daughter's going to be fine," the doctor told her.

You could hear a sigh of relief all around the room.

"She has a mild concussion," the doctor continued, "and a fractured left leg. There's nothing to worry about, but we would like to keep her at the hospital overnight for observation."

"Can I see her?" Mrs. Putnam asked.

"Certainly. Would you care to follow me?"

Bonnie's mom nodded as they quickly moved out of the room and down the hall toward her daughter's room.

Sarah wanted to see Bonnie, too, but she knew this wasn't the time. This was a time just for mother and daughter. Besides, there were other matters that Sarah had to attend to . . . like her own mother and father. It wasn't going to be pleasant, but it had to be done.

Meanwhile, back at home, Nicholas and McGee were facing their own unpleasantness. . . .

The dastardly dinosaurs were drooling all over their delectable delicacy . . . me—Caveman McGee! We'd been playing a pretty intense game of "Run for Your Life or We'll Gobble You Up!" Now that they had me cornered, it looked like I was it . . . in more ways than one.

Suddenly I started to really hate this game.

Now don't get me wrong, it had nothing to do with the dinosaurs. I mean, some of my best friends are dinosaurs. Why, just yesterday I had ol' Stegosaurus and my good pal Tyrannosaurus Rex over for some chips and dip while we caught a game on the ol' tube. I tell you, that Tyrannosaurus is a real crack-up. During halftime, he talked about this new invention of his called "fire." He said he could use it to cook things and to keep himself warm at night. Yeah, right. Like, I'm going to throw out my microwave and electric blanket to try some crazy new invention of his.

Right now, though, I would have traded just about anything to get out of this predicament. I mean, you could tell by the starved look in these Brontosaurus bullies' eyes that they were wondering if I had any taste. And we aren't talkin' about whether I like Picasso or not.

"Nicholas . . . ," I said calmly, showing my courage even in the face of annihilation. "NICHOLAS!!"

But instead of coming to the rescue, my little buddy just reached his hand down and ripped off the sheet of paper to start again. I managed to jump from the old piece to the new one just before

61

he crumpled it and tossed it into the trash. Poor Brontosaurus babies. And we were getting to be such good friends.

Still clad in my animal skins, I was now at the head of a giant ship. Only this time I was wearing a helmet with a set of horns that would turn Rudolph's nose green with envy.

Yes, it was I, Victor the Viking—obviously off to discover America.

I glanced to the left. Nothing was happening.

I glanced to the right. Nothing was happening.

I nervously cleared my throat and waited. Any minute ol' Nicky-boy would come up with some super fantasamagorical adventure in which I would be the star hero. . . .

Nothing.

Ahem. "Any minute now ol' Nicky-boy will come up with some super fantasamagorical . . . "

I said, "ANY MINUTE NOW OL' NICKY-BOY WILL COME UP—"

"I don't think so, McGee."

"What?"

"Not tonight," Nicholas repeated.

Hmmm . . . This was sounding serious. With a victorious vault that only valiant Vikings can vault, I leaped from the sketch pad and onto Nick's drawing table. "What's up, Buckaroo?"

"I don't know," he sighed. "It's this whole art table thing."

"Oh that," I said, nodding a knowing nod.

"I have to make a decision by tomorrow, and I still don't know what to do."

"Did you make up that list?"

"Yeah."

"How'd it come out?"

"Not so good."

I waited in silence. Sometimes even valiant Vikings are at a loss for words.

"I've tried everything I know," he said, sighing as he set his chin on the table. "And I still don't have an answer."

"Everything?" I asked. "Even what your parents suggested?"

He looked up to me (which is hard to do when someone's only seven and a half inches high). "You mean . . . prayer?" he asked. "You think God's just going to come down out of the sky and write the answer on the wall?"

"If he did your Mom would sure get mad. She just painted it last month and—"

"So if he doesn't write it out for me," Nick interrupted, "how am I going to know what he wants?"

"You got me, Bub. But you'll know. Somehow, you'll know."

Nick stared at me a long moment. I could tell by the look in his eyes that he knew I had a point. Then, before I knew it, he had his head bowed. I couldn't tell what he was saying, but by the way his lips were moving I knew he was getting serious . . . real serious.

And I knew an answer would be coming.

SEVEN
Monday . . . At Last

Monday took forever to roll around. Now we all know you're supposed to hate Mondays. It's like a law or something. Normally Sarah and Nicholas are pretty good at obeying that law. But this Monday was an exception. They couldn't wait for this Monday to happen.

Nicholas's reasons were simple.

Monday was the last day to make his decision about the art table. He was so tired of going back and forth, trying to make up his mind, that now he almost didn't care what decision he made—just as long as he made one.

Sarah's reasons were a little different.

I mean, first there was Saturday night and the ride home with her parents from the hospital. It was a very silent ride. But that was OK. Sarah didn't feel much like talking, anyway.

Then there was that night's sleep. Well, OK, so "sleep" isn't the right word. I mean, every time she managed to close her eyes she saw that green car and her friend sailing over the back end . . . or the blood from Bonnie's head on her pants . . . or Jason's bored glance at her . . . or even, even that stupid green Gummi Bear that had stuck to her pant leg. Then, once she had seen those pictures a billion times, they started mixing up with each other. Now she was holding her own bleeding head, or Jason was being hit by the car (which actually looked like a huge green Gummi Bear). On and on it went like this, through the whole night.

Then came Sunday morning. Over breakfast, a very droopy-eyed Sarah finally worked up the courage to ask what her punishment would be. Unfortunately, Mom and Dad said they hadn't decided yet. Now, to anyone who's ever been a kid, that only meant one thing: it was going to be bad news. Real bad news.

Then there was Sunday school. Of course, the whole subject of the morning was—you guessed it—disobedience. If Sarah hadn't known better, she would have bet her parents had called the teacher in the middle of the night and told him what to teach on. Talk about feeling miserable. I mean, all the poor girl could do was sit and fidget and look at her watch, and sit and fidget, and then fidget some more.

Then came Sunday afternoon. And her parents' decision. We're not talking just any old decision here. We're talking the worst possible of all decisions.

Sarah had just opened up the lid to the washing machine. Try as she might, she couldn't hold back a groan. This was the second time she'd put her new white pants through the wash cycle, and it was the second time they had come out stained. She wasn't sure if it was the mud and oil from the ground, or the Gummi Bears, or the blood—or a combination of all three. But whatever it was, the stain just wouldn't come out.

"What's up?" Mom had asked as she poked her head in the doorway.

"Oh, it's these stupid pants. I can't get this spot out."

"Let me see."

There had been an uneasy silence between the two as Mom looked over the stain. Sarah had still been feeling pretty guilty about the night before. She knew she'd really let her folks down and that it might take forever to regain their trust again. If you really get down to it, that's what bothered Sarah the most: that she'd lost her folks' trust.

After another long look at the stain, Mom had begun to talk. "Your father and I have been doing a lot of thinking. You know, about your discipline for last night."

Sarah had quietly braced herself for the worst. Unfortunately she'd had no idea how bad the worst could be.

Mom had continued. "We've decided that because of the seriousness of your disobedience . . . the lying, the deception, the blatant rebellion . . . "

Uh-oh, here it comes.

"And because you want to be treated as an adult . . ."

Sarah had slowly closed her eyes and waited.

"Well, we've decided that you're going to have to come up with your own discipline."

Sarah's eyes had popped open. *How could this be? How could she be so lucky?*

Well, at least that was what she had thought at first. . . .

But over the next few hours it hadn't taken Sarah long to realize she wasn't as lucky as she had figured.

At first she dreamed up some drastic discipline, like having to miss all of Grandma's overcooked vegetables for the next three months. Or being forbidden from talking to her pesky little brother for a week. Or, horror of horrors, having to have her own telephone installed in her bedroom.

But her folks wanted her to look at the decision like an adult. And when she started to do that— when she began to really understand the seriousness of her actions—well, suddenly, things weren't quite so easy.

Over and over again, she ran what she had done through her mind. Over and over again, she thought of what *could* have happened. And over and over again, she thought of the different punishments she should face.

Mom had given her until Monday to come up with a decision. But, like Nicholas, Sarah had grown so tired of running the choices back and forth in her mind that she almost didn't care what the punishment would be. Just as long as Monday would hurry up and come. Just as long as she could hurry up and get it over with.

Now, finally, it was here!

At precisely 8:23 A.M. Nicholas was sitting in his classroom sketching another McGee adventure as they all waited for their teacher, Mrs. Harmon, to arrive. Renee was looking over his shoulder and having a good laugh over what he was drawing.

"You know," she chuckled, "it's hard to believe you really make that stuff up."

Nick nodded. Sometimes he even surprised himself.

"So why don't you ever act as funny as McGee?" she asked.

Suddenly he stopped nodding. Now he wasn't sure if that was a compliment or not. But, whatever it was, it started him thinking.

Uh-oh, it's decision time again. Let's take a look and see what's going through the little guy's mind this time.

QUESTION: "WOULD I BE MORE POPULAR
IF I ACTED LIKE McGEE?"

Hmmm . . . Well, my answer is a definite yes! But, for the sake of science and considering all the angles, let's just press these buttons here, load in the Imagination Program and . . . All right, who let their Gooey-Nut Bar melt all over the Synaptic Crystals? How do you expect anybody to make clear decisions when his mind's full of all this sugary garbage? This sticky, gooey, yummy, scrumptious, knock-your-socks-off, incredible-tasting garbage?

Well, I suppose somebody has to clean up this mess. So . . .

SLURRRRRRP.

Burp!

68

Ahhhhh . . . much better. Now, where were we? Oh yes, the Imagination Program. Let's drop it in and take a look.

Check it out—there's Mrs. Harmon coming into the classroom. Let me turn up the volume a little.

"All right, class. Who would like to give their book report first?"

Now she's looking over the kids. Wait a minute! Something's wrong. She looks like she's seen a ghost. No, it's not a ghost, it's . . . it's . . .

"Nicholas?" she asks, looking slightly stunned.

Sure 'nuff, it's Nicholas. Only now he's the best-looking Nicholas you've ever seen. From his red high-tops and yellow/orange suspenders, to his blond hair combed up just like mine, he looks like . . . like . . . Hey, ya know what? He looks like me! No wonder he's so handsome, so dashing, so incredibly well dressed, and . . . did I mention handsome? Well, well, well—the kid's trying to be me!

Now he's leaping to his feet.

"That's my name" *he's answering Mrs. Harmon,* "don't wear it out—yuk, yuk, yuk." *Not exactly a great imitation of my incredible comic genius but, hey, at least the kid's trying.*

It must not be too bad a try, 'cause the rest of the class is just sitting there, staring in amazement.

"So what d'ya say, Teach," *he's asking.* "Can I get started on the old review-a-roo?"

Mrs. Harmon seems to be speechless, too. In fact, it's all she can do just to nod her head.

OK, let's fast-forward this a little and see what happens.

BREE-LEEEEEEEEEEEE . . .

Ah, here's the class again. Hmmm, their mouths are still hanging open. There's Nick in front of them. Hold it a minute. Not only is he giving his book report, it looks like he's playing one of the characters—complete with plastic sword and eye patch!

"Harr, Matey . . . shiver me timbers. Batten down me hatches, hoist the mainsail, and all those other kinda salty sayings. If ya don't tell me where ye've hidden me treasure, I'll have yur head, or my name ain't Long John Underwear, er, Long John Silver. Har-har-har."

Hold the phone! Look at those kids' faces! That's not amazement—that's distaste, that's disgust, and . . . oh no, could it be? Say it isn't so! But yes, yes, it's the worst of all possible things! That actually looks like boredom on their faces!

Can you believe it? Me, boring?? Me, the incredible, one-and-only McGee? I know it's only Nick trying to imitate me, but still . . . an imitation of me is better than no me.

Then again, maybe that's the problem. Maybe there's only room for one "one-and-only" me. Sure, it's great my little buddy wants to be like me. (And why not? How could you ask for a better role model?) But still . . . maybe he should just try staying himself.

"To McGee or not to McGee," that is the question. Well, by the expression on the kids' faces it looks like they already have the answer. So does Mrs. Harmon. Even Nicholas is starting to get the point. What's that he's saying?

"Come on guys, these are jokes . . . they're supposed to be funny."

No sale. The kids aren't buying it. In fact they look more boringly bored than before.

"What are you guys? An oil painting?"

Hmmm, I see their point. That may be one of my favorite lines, but even I can see how Nick is kind of . . . I hate to admit it . . . obnoxious. I mean, let's face it, this thing just ain't flying. Nick's definitely caught on to the fact, too. Look at that, he's even starting to sweat a little. Yes-siree-bob, I'd say our boy blunder's had enough, wouldn't you? (I know I have.) So let's go ahead and punch the Decision Button.

CONCLUSION: "DON'T BE SOMEONE ELSE. . . . BE YOURSELF!"

I'll eat to that. Now where'd that Gooey-Nut Bar go?

EIGHT
3:37 P.M.

On the way home from school, Sarah thought she'd swing by Bonnie's to see how she was. Bonnie had been released from the hospital Sunday afternoon. But she hadn't made it to school today. From what Sarah saw as she entered her friend's bedroom, it looked like she wouldn't be making it to school for quite a few days.

"Hi," Sarah said as she came in.

Bonnie turned from the trillionth rerun of "Gilligan's Island."

"Hi, yourself," she mumbled.

Sarah barely heard. She barely noticed Bonnie had spoken. What she did notice was how bad Bonnie looked. I mean, it was more than the huge bandage over her forehead, or the cast on her leg, or the throbbing headache she kept complaining about. It was even more than the bedpan she had to keep nearby to throw up in . . . something she'd been doing a lot of.

The fact is, Bonnie looked just plain bad. No

question about it. I mean, if you didn't know any better you would have thought she'd been hit by a car or something. Which makes sense, since she was.

Sarah tried to put on her best smile. You know, the type where you're trying so hard to look happy that you're not even sure what the other person is saying?

It took a little doing, but Sarah finally was able to cheer Bonnie up a little. Maybe it had something to do with them getting down to the important information. You know, like who is mad at whom, who's going with whom, and, of course, who Mr. Seneca—the awesomely handsome and incredibly single English teacher—is currently dating. You know, important stuff like that.

But during the whole conversation, one thought kept haunting Sarah. She just couldn't shake it. No matter what she said or how she said it, the thought just kept coming back to her: *This could be you lying in this bed.*

It was nearly an hour before their conversation died down. Bonnie was getting tired and needed some rest. At last, Sarah was able to leave. Of course, she promised to swing by again. And, of course, she'd be happy to drop off Bonnie's homework. But when Sarah finally stepped outside, it was like a breath of fresh air—like she could finally breathe again.

Yes, that could have been her in that bed. OK, so her parents set up some rough rules. Sometimes they seemed impossibly strict. But they had their reasons . . . like making sure she didn't end up like Bonnie.

Sarah sighed. So the rules had a reason for being there. Now all she had to do was think up the right punishment for not following them. . . .

"Hey, what's the big rush?" Louis asked as he and Nick left the school and raced for the bike racks.

"I'm going over to Graham's art store," Nicholas answered.

"So, you gonna make up your mind about the art table?"

"Yeah," Nick sighed as he started dialing the combination on his lock, "one way or the other. You want to come along?"

"Oh, yeah," Louis grinned as he popped the lock off his own bike. "Sounds like nonstop action to me."

Nick grinned back. He knew that deciding on a new art table didn't rate real high on Louis's Things-I-Just-Have-to-Do-Before-I-Die list. But he also knew Louis was a friend. And because it was important to Nick, it would be important to Louis. "Race you!" he shouted as he pushed off on his bike.

"You're on!" Louis shouted back as he hopped on and followed.

Meanwhile, Sarah was up in her room when she heard a gentle knock on her door. *Uh-oh*, she thought. *Here it comes.*

"Sweetheart . . . " It was Dad. "Can you come on downstairs a minute? Your mother and I want to talk to you."

"OK, Dad," Sarah answered. She tried to sound

as cheery as possible . . . considering she was heading for her own execution.

The trip down the stairs seemed to take forever. When she rounded the corner, it was just as she expected. There were her parents sitting in the family room, waiting. Mom was folding laundry. Dad had been reading the paper.

"Well," she sighed under her breath. "Here goes nothing."

At first they talked a little bit about school. Then a little bit about Bonnie. Finally they got to the real reason for the little pow-wow.

"So . . . ," Dad asked. "Have you reached a decision about your discipline?"

"I think so," Sarah nodded. Her voice croaked just a little. It was funny, but she almost sounded like Nick when he was nervous. She looked at her parents. They waited in silence. Then, taking a deep breath, she began.

"What I did was wrong. I mean, everything about it was wrong. I lied about going to Bonnie's, I disobeyed about going to the races. I mean, everything. It was . . . it was just all wrong."

She glanced up at her parents.

They waited in silence.

"And . . . " She swallowed, then continued. "Well, I think maybe grounding me for," she hesitated a second. This was going to be harder than she'd thought. "Grounding me until Christmas vacation, well, I think that would teach me my lesson."

Mom and Dad exchanged glances. More silence. Finally Dad spoke. He looked a little concerned.

"Honey . . . Christmas vacation is more than two months away."

Sarah could feel her eyes starting to burn. Any moment the tears would spill onto her cheeks. "Daddy, I know it should be longer, but I really wanted to go to the basketball tournament this year. Maybe, maybe after the tournament we could go back to grounding me, you know, until . . ."

"No, Sweetheart, that's not what we meant," her mom quietly interrupted. For a second Sarah thought she saw just a trace of a smile.

"You've obviously thought this over pretty carefully," Dad said.

"Yes, sir."

"You've thought about all of the rules you broke, and all of the reasons we made those rules."

"Yes, sir," she repeated.

"Well," he said, glancing toward Mom for agreement. "I think two and a half months is a little tougher than what we had in mind."

At first Sarah couldn't believe her ears.

"You see, Sweetheart," her mom joined in, "we don't punish you to make you suffer. We just want to give you a discipline strong enough that you'll remember . . . to teach you so you'll learn."

Dad continued, "The very fact that you took so long to think over your discipline . . . well, that by itself must have been a pretty strong lesson."

"One of the toughest," Sarah agreed with a long sigh.

Mom and Dad exchanged smiles.

"That's what we were hoping for," Mom admitted.

Sarah's heart was starting to race. This was

getting too good to be true. It was like some fairy tale with an and-they-lived-happily-ever-after ending. "So you mean," she asked excitedly, "that my making the decision was enough? Now I'm off the hook! No punish—"

"Not quite, young lady," Dad interrupted.

Sarah frowned slightly. Well, so much for fairy-tale endings.

"I think, though, that being grounded for four weeks should be enough," Dad finished.

"And no telephone privileges," Mom threw in.

Sarah's heart sank a little, but not much. I mean, let's face it, four weeks was a far cry from two and a half months.

"Thanks, guys," she exclaimed. And before she knew it, she was once again in their arms. First Mom's, then Dad's.

"Listen," Mom said. "Old moneybags here," she gave a poke at Dad, "promised to take us out to dinner when Nick gets home from the art store. Why don't you go change clothes?"

"Into what?" Sarah frowned. For a moment the dark cloud of gloom she'd been walking under for the past couple of days returned. "I spent all my money on those white pants, and now I don't have anything to wear."

"Not quite," Mom smiled. She reached over to the pile of laundry she'd been folding and produced the pants. "Why don't you try these?"

Sarah couldn't believe her eyes as Mom handed the white pants to her. "Look at this!" she cried as she turned the pants over and over in her hands. "The stain's completely gone! How'd you do it?"

"Experience," Mom said grinning.

"They're perfect!" Sarah held them against her. They looked great—as clean and new as when she first bought them. "Thanks, Mom!" She gave her mom another hug and whirled around toward the stairs.

"Though your sins are as scarlet," Dad quoted softly, "they'll be white as snow."

"What's that, Dear?" Mom asked.

But before Dad could answer—in fact, before Sarah had even reached the stairs, Nick suddenly barged into the room.

"Well, Kiddo," Dad asked. "What's the verdict? Did you get it?"

"Get what?" Nick asked.

For a moment everyone came to a stop. They looked at each other. Then in perfect unison they shouted, "The new drawing table!" (Though Sarah was the only one that added the phrase "idiot child" at the end.)

"Oh, that." Nick couldn't help but break into a grin. "Not exactly," he answered. And with that he reached into his backpack and pulled out a new tablet. "I decided to buy a sketch pad instead."

"But why?" Sarah asked in astonishment. "I mean, all week you've been talking—"

"I know, I know," he interrupted. "I just . . . I guess I just realized that a table like that was . . . well, I'm not really ready for something so fancy."

Everyone stood in silence as he continued.

"I got to thinking about all the time it took me to make that money, and the other things I could do with it—like buy a bike or help other people and stuff."

Mom and Dad were more than a little surprised
. . . not to mention pleased. Come to think of it, so
was Sarah. Being the older sister, it was her job to
look for opportunities to use little brothers to little
advantages. And right now, she thought she spot-
ted one of those ways.

"You know, Nicky, old friend," she said as she
lovingly put her arm around him.

Nick glanced at his parents. *"Nicky, old friend?"*
What was this all about? They were supposed to
be brother and sister. That meant nonstop war two
weeks past forever. What was this "Nicky, old
friend" stuff?

It didn't take long to find out.

"Maybe," Sarah continued, "just maybe you and

I should go in together to buy a car. . . ."

"A car?" Nick's voice cracked.

"Sure! What better way to spend that money?" She was guiding him toward the stairs. "I mean, I get my permit next year and everything. Now of course you wouldn't be old enough to drive right away, but I'd take care of it for you and you could ride in it sometimes and—"

"Sometimes?" Nick protested.

"Well, it's only fair. I mean, I don't want to chauffeur some little kid all around—"

"Who are you calling a kid?"

"Well, you're certainly not Mr. Maturity. I mean, look at that shirt, those pants."

"What's wrong with these . . . ?"

The rest of the argument was lost as the two headed up the stairs.

Mom and Dad glanced over to each other.

Things were finally getting back to normal.

NINE
Wrapping Up

Thus ends another fun-filled, all-expense-paid jour-
ney (except for the bucks you laid out for this book)
into the life and times of one Nicholas Martin, K.E.
(Kid Extraordinaire).

Hey, it's been a kick. A real slice. I'll tell you one
thing, I've decided decisions are tough customers.
Sure, sure, no one said they'd be easy. And the
older we get the more we'll probably have to make
'em. So I guess it doesn't hurt to start practicing
now. . . . Right?

I did spot one trick I plan to use, though. It was
Nick's three-step plan of: Listen to advice, Make out
a list, and Check out what the Boss (better known
as "God") has in mind. I figure the last one's the
most important. I mean, when you think about it, I
suppose God's been around a couple of years more
than most of us. So it's no wonder he has some
pretty good ideas about things.

Anyway, I'm glad that's over with for now.
At least until the next time. And, hey, thanks for

stopping by the ol' Brain Screen Room. Now, watch your head as you go out, and be sure to shut the door behind you. It's pretty chilly out there and, as you know, I like to keep Nick full of as much hot air as possible.

So, to all you kids and kidettes . . . ta-ta, au revoir, arrivederci, and all that fancy "catch ya later" sort of stuff. We'll see you again for our next exciting, action-packed adventure—same McGee time, same McGee station. Hmmm, speaking of stations, I wonder if I can pick up "World Championship Wrestling" on this screen? . . . Maybe if I disconnect this red wire and twist it onto this green one—

ZZZZTT!!

Groan . . . anybody got some aspirin?